THE GOO[ ] D,

AND EVERYTHING ELSE

Contents

September

Monday, September 2

Dear Journal,
I thought fifth grade was going to be great, but it's only the first day of school and it's already a disaster! School is as crazy as ever and, to make matters worse, my parents just announced that my mom's going to have another baby. I can't believe it! I can hardly stand the little brother I already have – I don't want Mom to have another one! Things are crazy enough in the Burnett family without a screaming, crying, stinky baby to worry about all the time.

Obviously I can't talk to anyone in my family about this, so from here on out, YOU are going to know the real story about what is going on in this crazy family, at school, and even about my worst enemy, Geoff Nelson. Journal, I am going to give you the lowdown on the good, the bad, and everything else in the life of Sara Burnett. So here goes...

First, I should give you some background on the kind of day I had before my family dropped the baby bombshell on me.

Even though it was the first day back at school, horrible Geoff Nelson put a frog in the teacher's water glass today. On purpose. He's always doing awful things, like knocking over all the bikes in the bike rack or dropping his math book in the sink. Last year he "accidentally" scared the wits out of our principal, Mrs. Fellows, by blowing up and popping a plastic bag behind her. After she recovered, she said, "I think we have an appointment in my office, young man."

The awesome news is that I love my new teacher, Mrs. Wood. She's funny, smart, and so cool. I've never had a teacher in a wheelchair before. She let us ask all sorts of questions about it. At first I wondered how she'd be able to teach us, but by the end of the day, I'd forgotten all about it. In fact, when Geoff put the frog in her glass, she was so calm about it. She just said, "What's going on?" and went over to check it out. We cringed when the frog knocked the glass over and spilled water all over her books and papers.

Mrs. Wood cleared her throat and calmly stated, "Everyone settle down, okay? Geoff, I'll see you in the hall. NOW!" She went out the door.

Geoff just stood there for a minute. I think he was trying to figure out what would happen if he didn't go. Finally he shuffled out, too. As the door closed, we all hooted, "OOO-OOOH!"

"SHHHH!" My best friend, Steph Nichols, tried to calm everybody down. "We'll get in trouble, too!"

"What do you think she'll do to him?" I whispered. She shrugged.

When the door opened two minutes later, Geoff walked in trying to look cool, but you could tell underneath he was worried. Mrs. Wood followed him in, looking perfectly calm, cool, and collected. She smoothed her hair and said, "Let's look through the novels we'll use for our first reading assignment this year." Believe it or not, she wasn't mad or crabby the rest of the day. Now, that's my kind of teacher!

Every night, my family eats dinner together and discusses the day. And we sure had a lot to talk about tonight! Mom and Dad are always interested in what's happening at school (sometimes too interested). Mark is finally in kindergarten this year, so now he'll have some school stories to tell, too.

"So, Mark, how was your first day of school?" Dad asked between bites, giving Mom a wink. My parents never wink at each other. I figured Dad must have had something in his eye.

Mark scowled across the table. "It was terrible!"

"What do you mean?" Mom asked, winking back at Dad.

Mom and Dad were acting very weird. Before I could ask what was wrong with them, Mark answered, "We didn't get any homework. All we did was color. And the class is mostly girls. Yuck!"

I giggled, thinking that my class would have loved all those things.

Dad gave me that warning look. "What kind of homework did you expect, Mark?"

"I thought we'd write reports, like Sara! The teacher is treating us like we're little kids!" Mark said.

I couldn't stand it. "Mark, you are little kids! Kindies can't write reports. They can hardly write their names!"

"Well, I can write my name! I can even read books and look stuff up! So why won't Mrs. Oatmeal let me write a report?"

Mom looked confused. "Mrs. WHO?"

"You know, Mrs. Oatmeal. My teacher." Mark explained impatiently.

I started to laugh hysterically. "It's O'Neill, not Oatmeal!"

"Whatever!" Mark huffed angrily.

Mark is not your average five-year-old. He's been able to read

10

since he was three. That was when Mom and Dad told me he's gifted, which I soon found out means he's too smart for his own good, and mine, too!

"Well, Mark, don't be too hasty about judging Mrs. Oatmeal," Dad suggested with a smile. "She hasn't even had a chance to get to know you yet. Once she finds out how much you already know, I'm sure she'll let you do all those other things."

"But what about all the girls in my class? They are so... gross!" Mark let out a big sigh.

"What makes you think that? Sara's a girl, and she's not gross," Mom said.

Mark took a deep breath and before he could respond, I jumped in. "Wait till you hear what happened in MY class today! Geoff Nelson put a frog in Mrs. Wood's water glass!" When I began my story, Mom looked at her watch, then at Dad. I could tell they weren't even listening. My parents hate it when I tell a story – they just don't think my life is important!

At the end of my ten-minute frog story, Dad raised his eyebrows at Mom, and she just smiled at him. They didn't even comment on the worst Geoff Nelson story of all time! Usually they would give Mark and me a lecture about how we should never do the bad things Geoff does. I could NOT figure out what was going on.

Dad cleared his throat loudly. "Kids, your mother and I have some exciting news, too." He leaned back in his chair and smiled at us. Mom's face was all red, and she carried her plate over to the counter.

After the way my parents had been acting all evening, I was suspicious, but Mark had tons of happy ideas about Mom and Dad's news. "What is it? A trip to Disneyland? Are we finally getting our puppy? Do I get to take karate lessons?"

"No, no, nothing like that," Dad assured him with a chuckle. Mom continued to putter around in the kitchen.

I've never seen my parents act so weird. For a second, I had no idea what they were about to tell us, but then I remembered that Mom had had a doctor's appointment this afternoon. "Wait a minute!" I said slowly. "You're not going to go and have another baby, are you?"

Dad's face turned bright red.

Mark said loudly, "No way, Sara! I'm the baby of this family. Tell her, Dad. Tell her she's a blubberhead."

"Sara's not a blubberhead," Dad said. He didn't say anything about the baby thing.

Mom came over with four bowls of ice cream. For the first time in my life, I didn't want dessert. Why do they need another kid when they already have Mark and me?

I realized Mom was speaking. "...and Dr. Spence said I'm due at the end of May. What do you think about a new brother or sister?"

Mark is SO rude! "Well, it better be a boy. If it's another girl, I don't want it. Can you send it back?"

Mom looked over at me. I knew I should be more polite than Mark, so I tried to think of a better answer, but... "It'll just cry and poop," I predicted. "We won't get any sleep, and we'll spend our lives changing a million stinky diapers! Anyway, do we have enough money to have another kid? Will you have to quit your job? Will I have to share a room?"

Dad started to get irritated. "Sara, we appreciate your concerns. We've always taught you to think things through before making your decisions. But this was not your decision. Mom and I thought it through very carefully."

"But..." I interrupted.

Dad continued, "You'll all be about five years apart. You and Mark are old enough to help with a baby. We want you to be excited about this." He was calming down, but I was still upset.

"Well, I'm not," I muttered as I pushed back my chair, got up, and stormed away from the table.

As I ran up to my room, I heard Mark ask, "Is this chocolate chip ice cream?"

How could Mark forget about the baby so easily? He just doesn't get it. I threw myself down on my bed and fumed.

After a while, fuming got kind of boring. That's when I saw you lying on my desk, Journal, and I knew just what to do. I'm so glad that I have you to tell all this stuff to, Journal. And I'll be careful not to let Mark get his grubby hands on you, or he'd read all my secret thoughts. That would be TRAGIC! (I learned "tragic" today in the novel for my reading group. It's such an important word I just had to use it in this tragic situation!)

October

Monday, October 21

Dear Journal,
It's almost Halloween! We've all been talking about trick-or-treating and our costumes for days. I've changed my mind about six times, and I still can't decide what I'm going to be.

"What are you going to dress up as?" I asked Steph when we were on the playground. "We need to decide soon!"

She grimaced and said, "I want to be a mad scientist, but my mom wants me to wear my sister's princess costume. She says it's perfectly good, and she doesn't have time to make a different one this year."

"Parents are so frustrating sometimes," I said sympathetically. "Did you ask your dad if he would mind taking both of us out to go trick-or-treating?"

"Yeah. He said if it is okay with your parents, it's okay with him."

I laughed. "My mom said if it's okay with your parents, it's okay with her!"

Steph giggled. "Let's see if Jill and Kelly can go with us. Maybe you guys can spend the night at my house this Saturday so we can plan our costumes together."

"I'll ask my mom," I answered. "She'll probably say, 'If it's okay with Steph's parents, it's okay with me.'"

Our parents are so goofy!

Saturday, October 26

Dear Journal,
Today was maybe one of the worst days in my life – and to think it started so well!

Steph did decide to have a slumber party today, so I made it a point to get to her house early in the afternoon so we could start our serious costume-planning. The weather was so gorgeous, though, that we couldn't bear to stay inside. So Steph, Kelly, Jill, and I went to go play frisbee at the park.

Now, normally I am not the world's best athlete, but I love playing frisbee. I can't think of anything better than the thrill of running to catch it and feeling it drop into your hands.

Anyway, we were all having a great time, that is, until Geoff and his only friend, Mike, came along. Before we knew it, they were interfering with our game. We just tried to ignore them, but as usual that was impossible.

Steph, who was practically tackled by Mike, hurled the frisbee at me. "Get it, Sara!" she yelled.

I was concentrating so hard on catching it that I didn't realize that despicable

Geoff Nelson was right behind me. I made a spectacular leap and caught the frisbee.

At that instant, Geoff grabbed ahold of the frisbee and shouted, "Give me that!" I wasn't about to let him destroy our game so I held on for my life.

Before I knew it, we were involved in a major tug-of-war. With one last, desperate pull, I tore the frisbee from his grasp, twirled around to escape, and slammed face-first into a huge tree trunk.

"AAAAAAHHH!" I screamed, stumbling backward. It hurt so bad I thought my head had exploded! For the first (and hopefully last) time in my life I saw stars, just like they do in cartoons.

"Are you okay, Sara?" Steph ran up and grabbed my arm. "Your nose is gushing blood like a faucet!" Kelly and Jill ran over, too.

"I thigk I bwoke by faze," I sobbed, tears pouring down my face. I had the most disgusting taste in my mouth, like I was sucking on pennies. I spit to get rid of it, and a big red splot hit the sidewalk. I suddenly realized it was REAL blood. I looked down and saw that my shirt was totally soaked with it! It was so GROSS!

Jill pulled a tissue out of her pocket and tried to mop up the blood as it dripped off my chin.

"Ow! Thad hurds!" I cried.

Jill started to shout, "It's all your fault, Geoff!" He started to back away from her.

"Hey! Come back here!" Kelly then yelled. Geoff turned and ran.

Just then a neighbor came up and asked, "Are you all right?" She gasped when she saw me all covered with blood. "I'll go get your parents, Steph! Stay with her!" she shouted, then she ran off.

"I feel kind of dizzy," I moaned.

"Lay down," Steph said, pushing me to the grass. "You're still gushing!" More kids crowded around and stared down at me.

"Are you okay, Sara? Are you going to faint? Sometimes when people bleed too much, they faint, or even bleed to death! I hope YOU don't die or anything...," Steph was babbling.

"Stev!" I sobbed, then winced painfully. "Jus' let be bleed in peace!" My head was pounding like a drum in a marching band. I just lay there on the ground, bawling while blood and tears ran into my ears, and wondered what was going to happen to me. More and more people were coming up to see what all the excitement was about.

"Where's Mom? What's taking her so long to get the car over here?" Steph started asking. I tried to look around for the car, but that made me feel even dizzier, so I closed my eyes.

Suddenly I heard a car pulling up right near us. Doors slammed, and Steph's mom and dad pushed through the crowd and knelt down beside me.

"Give her some room, please!" Steph's dad said loudly. Then he looked down at me. "Oh, Sara, what have you done to yourself?"

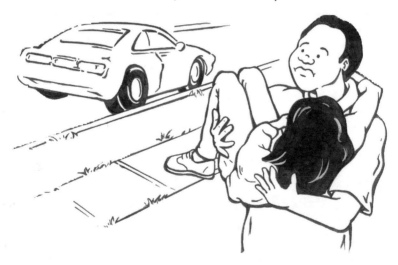

All I could do was cry in response.

"Don't worry, Sara, we'll get you fixed up in no time." Mr. Nichols picked me up and he and Mrs. Nichols set me gently in the back seat of the car. They let Steph come along to the hospital.

"Tell us what happened, Steph, we need to tell her parents," Mr. Nichols said.

Steph started telling the whole story. "See, we were playing frisbee with Jill and Kelly. Jill kept dropping the frisbee, and Kelly's throws are pretty wild, but we were still having a pretty good game. So anyway, we were just minding our own business..."

"Stev, be quiet! You're baking by head hurd," I complained.

"She's not making your head hurt. The tree did," Mrs. Nichols said. "Just close your eyes and rest until we get over to the hospital. Relax."

That sounded good to me, so I tried to take her advice.

When we got to the emergency room, Steph's parents called my parents and told them what happened and where we were. A nurse was taking my blood pressure while I was lying in an examination room, staring up at the ceiling. Soon another woman walked in. "I'm Dr. Hunt," she said. "I need to see how you are doing."

She flashed her little light in my eyes, in my throat, in my ears, and up my nose.

"I'm going to press on your face gently to see if your nose is broken. It might hurt a little," she warned.

Boy, did it ever! I think my scream helped convince her that my nose really was broken.

"We'll x-ray it just to be sure," Dr. Hunt said. "Can you walk across the hall?"

"Yeah," I said with a very small nod.

By the time I came out of the X-ray room, Dr. Hunt was talking to my mom. I was never so glad to see her in my life!

"Are you all right, honey?" Mom asked. "You look awful!"

"Thags a lod!" I said, feeling insulted.

Dr. Hunt chuckled, "She's right, Sara. You have a concussion and a lot of facial swelling. The X rays showed that there is a fracture to your nose, but luckily

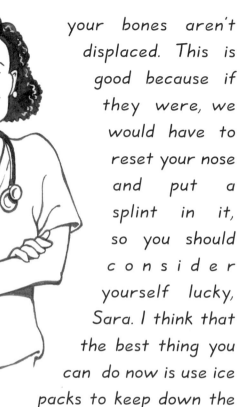

your bones aren't displaced. This is good because if they were, we would have to reset your nose and put a splint in it, so you should c o n s i d e r yourself lucky, Sara. I think that the best thing you can do now is use ice packs to keep down the swelling, and we'll give you something to take for the pain. In the meantime, since you've finally stopped bleeding, I think you can go home."

"Dr. Hunt," Mom asked, "is there anything else we need to know?"

"Well, Mrs. Burnett, there's a good chance Sara is going to wake up in the morning with a couple of black eyes."

25

I groaned when I heard the words "black eyes." I couldn't face the class with a broken nose AND black eyes on Monday morning. "How long do blag eyes last? Will dey be gone by Mudday?" I was afraid to hear the answer.

The doctor chuckled again. "I'm afraid they usually hang on for a good week to ten days, Sara. As for the blood stains on your clothes, try using cold water or hydrogen peroxide to remove them."

As Mom and I slowly walked out to the car, she started asking me questions. "How did this happen, Sara?"

"Geoff Delson did it! He's such a..." I yawned, which hurt a lot. "I cad't wait to go to bed. Whad dime is it?"

"Believe it or not, it's only eight-fifteen," Mom answered. "Don't fall asleep before we get to the car!"

So much for sleeping over at Steph's!

Mom and Dad helped me up to bed from the garage. I crawled in and grabbed you, Journal, so I could record all the gory

26

details of today. But it's almost ten and I'm SO tired... I'll get back to you later.

Sunday, October 27

Dear Journal,
The first thing I knew this morning, sunlight flashed across my pillow, piercing my eyelids. My head felt really heavy as I wiggled out of the covers, and I had to hold onto the railing on my way down the stairs. "Boy, what a night!" I muttered as I shuffled into the kitchen.

"Your voice is a little easier to understand today," Mom said, looking up from the newspaper. She jumped up to pull out my chair at the table. "Do you feel like eating?" she asked gently.

"You bet! I want a huge bowl of cereal and some cinnamon toast. I didn't lose my appetite, just a couple gallons of blood," I said. "If I were at Steph's right now, I'd be eating Mr. Nichols's world-famous sleepover pancakes."

Dad came downstairs into the kitchen, saw me at the table, and said, "Well, if it isn't Daddy's Little Boxer. Do you have anything to say to your loyal fans?" My dad is so corny.

"Daa-add," I moaned, "you're going to make me BMW!"

"Not that! Anything but that! It's too early for bawling, moaning, and whining," he said. "Seriously, Sara, is there anything I can help you with today? Do you have homework? Need a paper typed? Have to build a map of the fifty states?"

"No thanks, Dad. If I can just watch a whole lot of TV I'll be as good as new."

Both Mom and Dad were studying my face. "What's wrong with you guys?" I asked. "Quit staring at me!"

"Well, honey, it's just that...," Mom stopped as Mark came into the kitchen.

He took one look at me and said, "You look gross!" He snorted and plopped down into the chair next to mine.

"Yeah, and you look like something that crawled from under a rock," I said quickly.

Mark laughed so hard he almost fell out of his chair. "No kidding! Go look in the mirror, Sara!"

I hurried to the bathroom mirror and looked at a swollen face I didn't even recognize. "Aaaahhh!" I screamed.

My nose was the size and color of an eggplant. But that wasn't all. My eyes were beyond black. "This is a nightmare!" I thought, prodding the purple bags under my eyes. That was a big mistake. "Aaaahhh!" I screamed again.

"Sara, don't rub your eyes like that! Let's get more ice packs on them like Dr. Hunt suggested," Mom said.

"What am I going to do, Mom? I can't go to school looking like this!" Tears gushed from my swollen raccoon eyes.

Mom led me back to the kitchen. "We'll cross that bridge when we come to it. In the meantime, let's make some ice packs."

One other thing happened because of the tree problem. My dad talked to Geoff's dad about what Geoff did to me. His dad told my dad to jump in a lake. I guess like father, like son. Someday, Journal, I'm going to get back at that BLUBBERHEAD!

Monday, October 28

Dear Journal,
Of course Mom and Dad made me go to school today. It was totally humiliating to face everyone with my swollen face and black eyes - even worse than I thought! All the boys laughed like crazy when they saw

30

me. And Geoff calls me "Raccoon" all the time. I am suffering because of him and he gets to call me names. I can't believe it!

I guess the only good thing about the situation is that I finally know what I am going to be for Halloween. I'm going to go as a monster. A black-eyed, purple-nosed, puffy-faced monster.

November

Monday, November 11

Dear Journal,
Well, the black eyes are starting to fade, and otherwise things are calm... except for Jill, who always makes life interesting. She loves to sneak up on people when they're just coming out of the bathroom stall and shriek, "Surprise!" In fact, she'll do it to any

girl who goes into the bathroom, even the little kindies! We don't see what's so funny. That's Jill, though. She doesn't worry about losing friends if it means that she gets to laugh at you.

That's something I don't get. Jill isn't a good friend – she tells secrets, laughs at problems, and plays tricks on you every chance she gets. But she's still part of "The Crowd" – you know, my circle of friends. I don't know if Jill thinks it's cool to be mean, or what. I just try to stay out of her way.

Friday, November 15

Dear Jill, Jill, and More Jill Journal,
We're learning about alliteration in writing. Can you tell? Anyway, today Jill figured out that she can climb up and swing on the bathroom doors. Scaring people isn't good enough, now she's got to show off, too!

Once the rest of us saw Jill's new trick, we HAD to try it. Every time we go to the bathroom (which is much more often than usual – I wonder if Mrs. Wood has noticed), we practice climbing up and swinging on the doors. It's kind of like being a trapeze artist, only you swing on a door instead of a trapeze.

Some of the girls are pretty scared to swing. The truth is, I'm kind of chicken, too. I know I'm either going to fall off and land on my head, or break the door off. How'd you like to be known forever as "the girl who hit her head on a toilet"?

I don't think Steph wants to do it either. She tried it, but then she got down and hung around the trash can. She and I should just tell Jill we won't do it. What if we get caught? That would be the worst! Dad always says, "If you're in trouble at school, you're in trouble at home."

I need to quit worrying so much. No one will catch us. Teachers never use the students' bathrooms.

Monday, November 18

Dear Juvenile Delinquent's Journal,
I just reread what I wrote last Friday. I am such a blubberhead! If only I'd listened to myself, I wouldn't have gotten myself into this big, ugly mess.

34

You see, this afternoon, Jill, Kelly, Steph, and I ended up in the bathroom at the same time. Mrs. Wood obviously turned her teacher radar off for just one second, and we jumped at the opportunity.

When I walked into the bathroom, Jill was already swinging back and forth like crazy. Kelly was just pulling herself up, and Steph was leaning against the trash can, inspecting the dirt under her fingernails.

I didn't want any of Jill's grief about being scared to swing, so I was boosting myself up when I heard the familiar click-click of high heels and the boom of a grown-up voice. "And what are you girls doing?" the voice demanded. I froze where I was, hanging on the door, hoping Jill and Kelly could get us out of this mess. But it was completely silent out there.

"I could hear you laughing and talking all the way down the hall. Get down from there immediately!" the voice commanded.

As I dropped down, I finally recognized that voice. It was Mrs. Thomas, the dreaded sixth grade teacher. When sixth graders find out they're going to be in her class, they cry and beg for mercy. No one wants to have Mrs. Thomas for sixth grade. And there she was, standing in the girls' bathroom, directing her drill-sergeant glare at us!

"Who is your teacher?" she demanded.

Kelly squeaked out, "Mrs. Wood."

"Fifth graders, hmmm? We'll shape you up if you make it to sixth grade, no doubt about it! This behavior is totally inappropriate. You could have injured yourselves or damaged school property. I expect you to march straight to your classroom and tell Mrs. Wood what you've been doing. I'll speak to her after school to make sure you've done so," she lectured. Mrs. Thomas gave us one last angry glare, made a perfect military turn, and clicked out of the bathroom.

Panic seized us. We couldn't tell Mrs. Wood we were swinging on the bathroom doors. We could handle it if she only got mad at us, but we knew she'd be disappointed in us, too.

When we finally got to our classroom, we shoved Kelly ahead of us to be the spokesperson.

"Mrs. Wood?" she whispered. "We had a little problem in the bathroom just now."

Mrs. Wood's head snapped up. She looked at us anxiously. "Are you girls all right? Is someone sick?"

"No, we're fine. We just did something really stupid and we have to tell you about it," Kelly mumbled. The rest of the class was no longer working. I could feel twenty pairs of eyes staring at us. I knew every ear was straining to hear our conversation.

"Go on, Kelly," Mrs. Wood said calmly.

"Mrs. Thomas caught us swinging on the bathroom doors, and she told us we had to

tell you what we were doing. She's going to check with you after school to make sure we told you. We're really sorry, and we won't do it again. I guess we just weren't thinking," Kelly blurted.

Mrs. Wood turned to Jill, Steph, and me. "Is there anything else I should know about this, girls?"

I spoke up. "Steph wasn't swinging, she was just watching us. I don't think she should have as bad a punishment."

"That's nice of you, Sara. Tell me, Steph, have you swung on the doors before today?" Mrs. Wood asked.

38

Steph nodded sadly. "But I only did it once because it seemed too dangerous."

Mrs. Wood nodded, looked up at the ceiling for a minute, and then told us we each had to write her a letter telling her what we thought a fair punishment would be, and why.

As I sat down, I wondered what punishment would be okay with Mrs. Wood for this kind of problem. Missing recess? Calling our parents? Sending us to Mrs. Fellows? No one had ever been caught swinging on the bathroom doors before. I had no idea what to write.

It took us a while to finish our letters. Jill got done first and took hers to Mrs. Wood. I watched her intently all the way there. Mrs. Wood pointed to something in the letter, whispering to Jill. Jill nodded and went back to her seat. I was dying to know what was going on.

Kelly was next and followed the same steps as Jill. She gave me the "A-OK" signal as she went back to her desk.

When Steph finished her letter, she nervously walked to Mrs. Wood's desk and laid it down. Mrs. Wood read it slowly, gave Steph a quick smile, and whispered something in her ear. Steph smiled back, then headed for her seat.

I stood up to take my turn, relieved that all three of my friends survived. At that moment, the bell rang, and the class started packing up to go home.

Seeing the letter in my hand, Mrs. Wood said, "Sara, I need to speak to you privately. Can you stay after school?"

I nodded and sat back down. My stomach was doing back flips. I couldn't wait to get that letter out of my hand.

"Bet she calls your parents, Raccoon!" Geoff whispered as he walked by my desk.

I waited until everyone had left, then went to Mrs. Wood's desk. When I gave her my letter, I saw Mrs. Thomas walk through the door, coming to check up on us.

"Did my little friends do as they were told?" she asked, glaring at me.

Mrs. Wood nodded. "I was just going to listen to the letter Sara wrote me about the problem. Would you like to listen, too?"

I couldn't believe it. I was going to have to read my letter in front of Mrs. Thomas? This should have been my punishment!

I gulped and started reading:

"Dear Mrs. Wood,
I'm sorry I disappointed you today. I wish I'd never swung on the bathroom doors. It was so stupid. I thought a lot about what kind of punishment I should have, and I think it should be serious, because we set a bad example for younger kids, and we could have hurt ourselves or broken the doors. Here's my list of consequences:

1. Miss lunch recess and afternoon recess for the rest of the week.

2. Do an extra math assignment every day for the rest of the week.

3. Only go to the bathroom when we break for lunch every day for the rest of the week."

Mrs. Thomas gasped. "That seems pretty extreme, Sara," said Mrs. Wood.

"I tried to make it fit the crime," I said.

I couldn't tell what Mrs. Wood was thinking. "Is that the end?" she asked.

"Almost." I dreaded reading this part:

"Even though I know kids think Mrs. Thomas is mean, she was right to yell at us. When you do something wrong, you should get in trouble. If this isn't enough punishment, I could have other consequences, too. I know you won't be able to trust us anymore, and I'm really sorry. Sincerely, Sara Burnett."

I was terrified to look at Mrs. Thomas. I could feel her eyes burning into me, and I knew by the way she sat straight up she was really mad. I didn't blame her. If I were a teacher I'd be mad at me, too.

"Sara, your punishment will begin tomorrow. You can go now," Mrs. Wood said.

I grabbed my backpack and coat from the rack and hurried toward the door. As I went out, I thought I heard a giggle from the classroom. I walked around the building and peeked in the classroom window. Mrs. Wood and Mrs. Thomas were facing each other and giggling. I saw Mrs. Thomas pound on her leg, and then both of them exploded with laughter. What was so funny?

After dinner tonight, Steph called to ask how it went with Mrs. Wood. I told her my punishment, including how I had to read my letter to Mrs. Thomas.

"Wow, Sara! Why didn't you just turn yourself in to the police?" she asked.

"I'd rather go to jail than read that letter in front of Mrs. Thomas. What will I do if she is my teacher next year?" I moaned. "What punishment did you choose?"

"I have to miss two recesses," Steph said. I almost dropped the phone. Then she said that Kelly has to miss two recesses and write apology letters to Mrs. Thomas and Mrs. Fellows, and Jill's doing the same, plus picking up paper towels in the bathroom for two days.

I was so surprised I could barely speak. Suddenly I knew I'd overdone it. What was I thinking? Why did I ever think that I needed to suffer for my crimes? And now my buddies are getting off easy compared to me. It isn't fair.

Oh, Journal, there's only one thing to say, ARRRGGHH!

Friday, November 22

Dear Journal,

IT'S FINALLY OVER! I survived my punishment, but it wasn't easy. I used my recess time to do the extra math assignments, so that part was okay. It was missing out on the four-square tournament at lunchtime that I hated.

Today while I was working on my last extra math assignment, Mrs. Wood rolled over and asked me how I was doing. I told her the extra work had helped me understand triple-digit division better than any other math we'd learned this year!

She laughed, but then her face got serious. "Sara, I'm impressed with the way you've handled yourself this week. You took full responsibility for your actions, and you didn't try to blame someone else. You chose a heavy punishment, and you followed

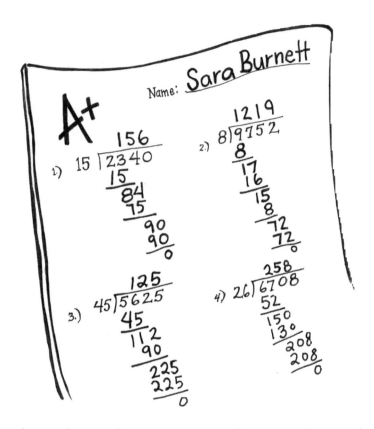

Name: **Sara Burnett**

A+

1.)
$$15\overline{)2340} = 156$$
15
84
75
90
90
0

2.)
$$8\overline{)9752} = 1219$$
8
17
16
15
8
72
72
0

3.)
$$45\overline{)5625} = 125$$
45
112
90
225
225
0

4.)
$$26\overline{)6708} = 258$$
52
150
130
208
208
0

through without one single complaint. I almost told you your punishment was too severe, but if I had, I think you'd have lost an important chance to grow. What did you learn from this experience, Sara?"

I couldn't believe what she was saying to me. "Well, I was right when I thought we shouldn't swing on the bathroom doors."

"And?" Mrs. Wood asked.

46

"I should have stood up to Jill. Steph did, but I was afraid to."

"I think those lessons were worth every bit of punishment you chose for yourself. You'll learn to trust your conscience. You're going to have to make lots of tough choices as you grow up, some of them tougher than this one. I don't say this to all my students, but I trust you to make the right choices."

I don't exactly get what Mrs. Wood meant, but I can tell she was giving me a big compliment. I'm really going to have to think about this for awhile. I wonder if Mrs. Wood said the same things to Steph, Kelly, and Jill.

December

Sunday, December 21

Dear Jingle Bell Journal,
This morning I realized I had no money to buy presents. I should have saved some. I probably didn't HAVE to go to the movies with Steph last Friday. And I didn't need the popcorn and candy I bought there, either. But it's too late now. My savings, all $18.67 of it, is gone forever.

I called Steph to see what she's giving her family. She's penniless and miserable, too. We decided to cheer ourselves up by going to the mall this afternoon with Mom.

But the mall is pretty depressing when you have no money! I saw tons of stuff I'd love to buy, but couldn't afford. And the more we shopped, the worse it got. I usually can't wait for Christmas. For the first time in my life, I was dreading it.

Then our luck began to change. It all started while we waited for Mom near the giant gingerbread house where Santa hears all those little kids' Christmas wishes.

While we waited, we watched hundreds of impatient little kids pushing and poking each other in a huge line. It went from one end of the mall to the other, and back again! "Geez! That's the biggest bunch of brats I've ever seen!" I whispered to Steph.

Steph agreed. "Someone should tell them that Santa won't leave any presents for the naughty kids."

I watched one little girl waiting in line near us who was doing the "potty dance," just like Mark used to when he needed to get to the bathroom quick. The girl's mother was holding on to three shopping bags and a stroller with a baby sleeping in it. The lady was saying, "If we get out of line to go potty, we'll lose our places. Then we'll have to go to the end of the line. Can't you wait a few more minutes?"

"NNNOOO!" the little girl whined.

A terrible thought crept into my head. "Mom and Dad will probably make me stand in line so the baby can see Santa. I'm doomed to a life as a built-in baby sitter."

Then, the next thing we knew, the little girl's mom was calling to us! "Say! Would you girls mind holding our place in line while I take my daughter to the bathroom?"

"Who, us?" I asked, looking behind me.

"Yes, you! We'll only be gone a few minutes, I promise, and the line probably won't even move," she said, trying to convince us.

"But my mom is waiting for us and...," I started to say.

"We have to go home," Steph said.

"Oh, thank you! I'll even pay you when we get back," the desperate mother said. We watched, speechless, as she wheeled the stroller around and dragged it and her little girl away.

We were SO embarrassed. I wondered how many more times we'd get stuck doing this before Mom showed up... Then it hit me!

I turned to Steph. "Hey! This gives me an idea! We could work as place-holders in the line. Parents could go to the bathroom, or shop, or do whatever they wanted until it was their kid's turn to see Santa."

"Yeah! We could call ourselves 'Steph and Sara's Sitter Service.' How much should we charge? We could make some signs and stuff..." Steph was off and running.

The mother, little girl, and baby came back, looking very relieved, and then the mother handed us two whole dollars for about five minutes of standing! I thanked her for the money and said to Steph, "See? This is gonna be great! Come on, let's go ask for permission!" I grabbed her arm and dragged her up the gingerbread steps to the front of the line.

"Hey, you can't cut in line! We've been waiting two hours," snarled the cranky dad who was next to see Santa. Little did he know we had the perfect idea to solve his problem!

Santa was suspicious of what a couple of ten-year-olds had to say, until I blurted out our idea. A gigantic smile slowly spread across his face as I explained about how we were trying to make some money during

our school vacations. Then he said, "Why don't you come back tomorrow morning at 10:00 when the mall opens? What a wonderful idea - ho ho ho!" Santa's huge laugh was the best thing we'd heard in a long time!

We left the gingerbread house and dashed to the bench, where Mom was waiting for us. "Hurry up, Mom. We've got work to do!" I said. We explained our plan as we dragged her along. Mom finally said, "I'm too tired to think about this. If it's okay with Mrs. Nichols, it's okay with me." We were halfway there!

By the time we explained our idea for the third time to Steph's mom, we were ready to burst with excitement. Mrs. Nichols was tough to convince, but when Steph told her it'd be a "Great Learning Experience," she finally gave in.

We had so much to do! First of all, we had to settle on how much to charge. We decided $2 for each job would be okay. It's easy to split fifty-fifty, and the desperate mother had given us that much without blinking an eye.

Finally, we tried to figure out costumes that would let people know we were

Santa's helpers. I had some red-and-white striped suspenders, but Steph didn't, and she insisted we should look exactly the same. We finally agreed on green turtlenecks and jeans: boring, but practical.

When I got home that evening, I was so sleepy I could barely talk to my parents. As Dad walked me to my room, he said Steph and I were real entrepreneurs. Then he offered me the money box he has in his workshop. The box will be perfect for our new parttime job.

I was so tired I wanted to go straight to sleep, but I just had to write this all down. It's the best idea I've ever had!

Tuesday, December 23

Dear Reindeer Report,
The last two days have felt like two weeks! Steph and I try hard to smile and be nice, even when they're hitting each other (the kids, I mean) or arguing about who was first in line (the parents, I mean). We go

home every afternoon and collapse into bed. I can hardly wake up to eat dinner or tell my family about my day, which is usually one of my favorite activities. I need to write down as much as I can so I don't forget our days as entrepreneurs.

The good news is that we're making tons of money. On the way home in the car each day, we open the money box and take turns counting. On Monday we made $68 and today we made $92 – it's just unbelievable! If we survive, we'll be rich!

Wednesday, December 24

Dear Mixed-up Memoirs,
Today has been one of the best days of my entire life. It's also been one of the WORST days. I don't even know where to start my story. It's just too outrageous. I can hardly believe I could be such a goofball.

Santa's Workshop was only open for six hours today, but it seemed like there were millions of people there finishing their last-minute shopping. By 4:00 we were more exhausted than we thought possible.

My dad was waiting for us at the gingerbread house when the workshop closed. We left quickly, glad our days in the work force were over!

As we drove home, it took Steph a long time to count all the dollar bills jammed in our money box. "One hundred! One hundred and five, ten, twenty... One hundred and twenty-four," Steph finally said. She looked at me with wide eyes.

"No way," I whispered.

"This is amazing," said Steph.

When we added up all three days, we had earned $284! Divided by two, it was $142 each!

"We'll buy some great presents now, won't we, Sara?" Steph laughed as she got out of the car and slammed the door.

Right then it hit me. My stomach did a flip and landed in my throat. I rolled down the car window. "Hey, Steph!" I yelled. "We never did our own Christmas shopping!"

She slowly turned around and looked at me. "No way," she whispered.

"I don't believe it!" I added.

"Now what?" Steph asked. Christmas lights reflected in the tears welling up in her eyes. "All that hard work, and we still don't have any presents for our families!" She stumbled up her front steps and disappeared inside.

When Dad and I walked into the kitchen, Mom was busy cooking Christmas Eve dinner. She turned around when she heard the door and I couldn't stand it another second. The tears erupted like a bursting dam, and I sputtered, "We were so busy working, we forgot to buy your presents!"

Mom and Dad sandwiched me in a hug. Mom said, "Sara, you thought up a wonderful, creative idea and followed through with it. That's the best Christmas present you could give us."

Dad added, "We're really proud of you!"

"It's all right, Sara," Mom continued. "Look on the bright side. Next week everything will be on sale, and you can get our presents cheaper! You'll have money left over to spend on yourself."

I hadn't thought of it that way. Maybe it will be okay after all.

Mom sent me upstairs to take a nap before dinner.

I sighed. "Don't forget to call me, or I'll probably sleep till New Year's!"

January

Sunday, January 5

Dearest January Journal,

Things have been pretty boring around here compared to all of that holiday craziness. Tonight we had a family meeting about the baby situation. Dad offered to give up his den for a nursery so neither Mark nor I would have to share our rooms. I was so relieved!

Mark piggybacked off Dad's idea, saying, "Since we never live in the living room, why don't we make it your den, Dad?"

Mom, the interior decorator, jumped on that plan. "Great idea! We'll build some bookshelves, make room for your desk, and get some big comfy chairs to read in!"

As for Mom's job, we came up with another great idea: After the baby is born,

Mom will still work for the interior design firm, but will do it from home. Her boss ought to like this idea, because she's afraid Mom will quit altogether.

I think it might be kind of cool to have Mom home more. Then if I forget my lunch or something, she can bring it to me. Hmmm.

Mom liked the idea, too. "I'll see if Nancy will let me try this, starting six weeks after the baby's born. That will give Baby Adrian and me a chance to get used to each other before the fabric starts flying."

"Baby Adrian?" Mark asked, making a face. "We're not naming it Adrian, are we?"

I was pretty worried about Adrian, too. How could I ever explain it to my friends? I'm not even sure how to spell it!

Mom's feelings were hurt. "Adrian was my grandfather's name. I've always dreamed of naming a child after him."

"That's not a dream, it's a nightmare!" I informed her. "And by the way, 'Adrian' doesn't work. No one will know if the kid's a boy or a girl."

"You never like any of the names I suggest, Sara! Do you have any better ideas?" Mom asked.

"Hmmm. I still like 'Egbert' best," I teased her. "But 'Sebastian' isn't too bad."

Mark hooted. "What about something extra crunchy, like 'Rocky' or 'Zoltan'?"

It was my turn to hoot. "Yeah, let's name the baby after a super hero!"

"Baby Zoltan"

"What about girl names?" Mom asked. "You know, I could have a girl, Mark. We can't name her 'Zoltan.'"

"No! No more girls! How many times do I have to tell you?" Mark shrieked, pounding his fist on the table. He's gotten more and more stubborn about this girl thing as Mom's stomach grows. I've never seen Mark act so crabby. Just wait until he realizes that he and the baby are going to share the same birthday month. He's going to hate it!

February

Tuesday, February 10

Dear Journal,

Well, it feels like we've been back in school forever again – our winter break seems like months ago. Thank goodness I have Valentine's Day to look forward to! It is absolutely, positively my favorite holiday (well, one of them, at least!), and I can hardly wait for our class party.

We decided to throw the party this upcoming Friday, and in addition to all the normal festivities, we're going to have a valentine mailbox contest for the prettiest, the funniest, and the most unusual mailbox. I can't wait!

As usual, Geoff the obnoxious tried to ruin things. "I'm not giving any valentines, so I'm not making a box!" he announced.

"Where will we put your valentines?" Mrs. Wood asked.

Before he could think of an answer, Mrs. Wood turned to the rest of us. "Geoff reminded me of my valentine rule. If we're giving valentines to one another, you must give them to everyone in the class. That way, we won't have hurt feelings."

We groaned so loudly Mrs. Fellows must have heard us all the way down in her office! Steph and I would've been perfectly happy not giving Geoff valentines. I'll hate him forever for making me run into that tree last October. Since then he never misses a chance to call me "Raccoon."

After Mrs. Wood's announcement, we planned three party committees. I'm on refreshments (with Jason – the cutest boy in the whole class! I can't believe my luck!). Steph's on decorations, and Kelly and Jill are on games. We'll make sure this is the perfect Valentine's Day party!

As we walked home from school today, Steph and I tried to figure out how we'll make our mailboxes. I think I'll try for the "prettiest" prize, but I doubt I'll get it. I never win anything. As usual, Steph has tons of creative ideas. I have none!

"I was thinking about using an oatmeal container. You know how they're round instead of square?" she said.

"Yeah! That'd be cool!" I said. "Maybe we could go to the craft store tomorrow and buy glitter and sequins and stuff to decorate them. Last time we were there, I saw all sorts of stuff that we could use."

At dinner I filled my family in on all of the plans for the Valentine's Day party. "I volunteered to bring heart-shaped cookies with pink and red frosting."

"I don't think I can stand up long enough to make them," Mom reminded me, patting her round tummy. "Little 'Evelyn' makes my legs ache when I'm on my feet."

"Don't worry, Mom, I'm happy to make them myself," I reassured her. Happy? Actually, I couldn't wait to get started on the party preparations!

66

Thursday, February 12

Dear Journal of a Great Mailbox Designer,
I've worked really hard to get everything ready for the party tomorrow!

Last night I baked the cookies, and my mailbox turned out incredible! I found the most perfect box (it's heart-shaped!) and I decorated it with tons of pink, red, and white ribbon, and lace and sequins. As an added touch, I sprayed glitter all over the whole thing, and Dad helped me cut a heart-shaped hole for the valentine envelopes. I've worked so hard I just know

I'm going to win! I wonder what Kelly got for the prizes – I hope they're really cool!

After dinner, I raced up to my room to get my valentines ready for the party. I got them out, dumped them all on my bed, and sorted them into three piles: "Boys I Don't Like," "Boys I Do Like," and "Girls." It took forever to write on the cards, put them in envelopes, drop in candy, and seal them shut.

Finally I had only two names left: Jason and Geoff. I also only had two valentines left. One said, 'Valentine, you make my day!' The other said, 'Be my valentine, or else!' I finally decided to give Jason the one that said, 'Be my valentine, or else!' I hoped he'd think it was funny – NOT serious.

That left only 'Valentine, you make my day!' for Geoff, my one true enemy in the world. Suddenly, I got a jumbo idea. On

the front of Geoff's valentine I added one word that changed the meaning of the whole valentine. Then I stuck it in its envelope.

Just as I finished, Mom poked her head in my doorway and told me it was time to go to bed.

I quickly wrote 'Geoff' and 'Jason' on the envelopes. I put a bunch of candy in Jason's envelope and none in Geoff's (ha ha!).

Friday, February 13

Dear Doom and Gloom Journal,
This morning the sky was gray and gloomy. Little did I know it was a forecast of my whole day! It all started out fine, sort of.

My mom tried to make heart-shaped pancakes for breakfast. She put red food coloring in the batter and used a pancake mold. Only she didn't wait long enough for the batter to cook, and when she picked up the mold, the batter turned into normal round pancakes. They looked like huge drops of blood. (Gross!) "Oh well," she sighed. "What do you expect on Friday the 13th?"

I hadn't even thought about that.

I made it to school without dropping anything. Unfortunately, that was the best part of my day. Mrs. Wood had a hard time keeping us under control all day, but finally party time arrived. It was fun to see all the different valentine mailboxes people had made. Some looked like the kids had spent five whole minutes on them, but others were really cool. I thought mine looked better than a lot of them. "Do you think I'll win 'Prettiest'?" I asked Steph.

"Definitely. Do you think I'll get 'Most Unusual'?" She'd used oatmeal containers to make a roller skate, and spray painted the whole thing fluorescent pink.

"Absolutely," I agreed. Why can't I think up ideas like that?

Our refreshment committee had gone crazy! There were pink and red cupcakes, red foamy punch, my cookies, pink jelly beans, and red licorice strings. Poor Jason was so embarrassed because his mom made him bring radishes with pink vegetable dip. She said the rest of us would only bring junk for the party. Sounds like something my mom would do!

We all stuffed ourselves with pink and red food. That was the second best part of my day. Before long, however, Geoff was holding his stomach and moaning, "Ooooh, I think I ate too much."

Mrs. Wood was at her desk, looking like she'd already had too much excitement. She asked, "Do you want to go see the nurse and miss the party?"

"No, I'm okay," he said. If only he'd gone to the nurse, my life would have been perfect!

We played lots of games and, as usual, I didn't win any prizes.

Finally Kelly announced, "Okay, it's time to judge valentine mailboxes! Raise your hand if you want to nominate a mailbox for Prettiest, Funniest, or Most Unusual. I'll make three lists on the chalkboard."

Kelly picked me first. "Sara?"

"I nominate Steph's for Most Unusual." It took a long time to get through the other nominations. In the back of the room, Geoff kept waving his hand and making noises so Kelly would notice him. "Oh... oh... oh..."

Mrs. Wood said, "Geoff, Kelly will be more likely to call on you if you sit quietly with your hand up."

"I don't want her to call on me! I feel sick, Mrs. Wood!" he said.

"Come up here so I can see if you have a fever," she said, sounding annoyed.

We all looked at him to see if he was faking, but his face was kind of pale as he walked up the aisle toward Mrs. Wood. Suddenly he stumbled next to my desk, grabbed onto it, and barfed all over my valentine mailbox.

I was totally stunned. I couldn't believe what it looked like.

I ran to the sink for some paper towels, but it was a lost cause. All my hard work destroyed in one second! Why did he have to barf on my mailbox? Life is so unfair!

I gave up and threw away my repulsive, smelly mailbox. It was ruined, my valentines were ruined, and so were my chances to win the prize for prettiest valentine mailbox. I would have felt much better if I could just curl up and die!

I couldn't get away from the smell of barf. It was everywhere!

Up at the front of the class, Kelly held her nose and went back to the chalkboard. "Okay, let's finish the contest. Are there any more nominations? Jason?"

Jason said, "I'd like to nominate Sara's mailbox for Most Unusual."

The class was dead quiet. I turned and looked at him. He winked at me and gave me the most adorable "poor you" face.

I was sure he could hear my heart thumping. Then everybody else cracked up, and finally, I had to laugh, too. Maybe there was life after barf!

At last I won a prize: Most Unusual valentine mailbox. It wasn't exactly what I'd planned, but it was better than nothing. At least, that was my first thought.

But the day's horrors weren't over! Steph walked up and glared at me. "I was supposed to win that prize!"

I didn't get it. "Are you mad at me?"

"Yes! You knew I wanted to win Most Unusual!"

"Oh, yeah, I planned the whole thing! I asked Geoff to barf on my mailbox just so I could beat you! You knew I was trying for Prettiest!" I protested.

"Yeah, right," she argued. She sat down, turned her back to me, and ripped open her valentines.

"Next year, ask Geoff to barf on your mailbox so you can win!" I snapped.

I sat in my seat and watched the clock, just waiting for the bell to ring an ending to this awful day.

Before it did, one last disaster found me. Jason came up and shoved a valentine in my face. "Very funny!" he said angrily. It was the card I'd made for Geoff that said, "Valentine, you make my day... rotten!"

"How'd you get this?" I asked.

"You put it in my mailbox. You even signed the back!" Jason said.

He was right. It said, "Sara."

"That was supposed to be for Geoff!"

"Sure," he said. "If you don't like me, just say so!" He stomped back to his seat.

Geoff barfed on my mailbox. Steph is mad at me. Jason thinks I hate him. Geoff's going to find Jason's valentine in his mailbox. This was Friday the 13th, all right. What a nightmare!

March

Monday, March 2

Dear Only-Friend-in-the-World Journal,
Well, it looks like I'm in for another awful Friday the 13th – that's right, my birthday actually falls on Friday, March 13. This morning Mom asked me who I want to invite to my party.

"Nobody. Nobody will come," I said gloomily.

"What's that supposed to mean?" she said.

"Remember Geoff Nelson and the whole valentine mailbox thing? Steph, Kelly, and Jill still aren't speaking to me," I answered.

"It sounds to me like you need some new friends," Mom said. "None of those kids has a good reason to be angry with you."

Mom doesn't get it. It doesn't matter if they have a reason to be mad at me. They just are! Steph is the one that surprises me the most. The only time she talks to me is when we have to work together on our social studies project. After we present it on Thursday, she won't talk to me at all!

Mom gave me a long lecture about how it was when she was a girl. She said she and her friends were mean to each other the whole time they were teenagers. She finally said, "Eventually my friends started treating each other better. It's like the Golden Rule says, 'Do unto others as you would have them do unto you.'"

"What?" I demanded.

"It means you should treat others the way you want to be treated."

"So I should be nice to them because I want them to be nice to me?"

"You've got it!" Mom pushed me toward the door. "Be a leader!" she called after me.

Yeah, right. She makes it sound simple. But I don't have any better ideas, so I guess I'll try the Golden Rule thing. I'll let you know what happens!

Tuesday, March 3

Dear Journal,

I got Steph to talk to me today, not like we used to, but more than she has been. I guess that Golden Rule thing sort of worked!

My plan was to pretend nothing was wrong and treat my friends just like I always do. I got to school and went to our normal line-up place.

Jill and Kelly were already there, whispering together. When they saw me in line, they looked at each other and giggled.

I pretended not to notice, and turned around to talk to Miranda about the social studies projects we were working on. Steph was right behind her, staring past us like we were invisible.

"Steph and I are doing Washington, D.C. She had a great idea about making a guide book for kids," I told her.

"That's extra crunchy!" Miranda said. "Steph always comes up with great ideas."

I nodded. "I'm glad she thought of it."

The bell rang and we went inside. As I emptied my backpack into my desk, Steph said, "Um, Sara?"

I tried to hide my surprise. "Yeah?"

"Is your part of the project going okay?"

"Yeah. Is yours?" I asked casually.

She nodded and sat down. Later Steph accepted my invitation to play four-square at recess. At least it was a start!

At dinner Mom asked me about my birthday party again. "Who do you want to invite, Sara?"

I've been thinking about this ever since. I guess I'll invite Steph, and I better ask Kelly and Jill, or they'll really be mad at me. I think I'll invite Miranda, too. She's been pretty nice to me lately...

Oh, by the way, Mom's now calling her stomach "Magnolia." I may not be excited about this baby, but I don't want to be dragging around some kid who is named after a flower! Mark still refuses to accept that the baby could be a girl. There's a fifty-fifty chance he'll be miserable! I hope it's a girl... I mean, since we have to have a baby and everything.

Thursday, March 5

Dear Journal,
Steph and I presented our Washington, D.C., project today. It went well, except for Kelly and Jill making faces at me. I just quit looking at them, and then it went fine.

I addressed and mailed my invitations tonight. Mom and Dad never let me pass them out at school, because they don't want me to hurt anybody's feelings. It's that Golden Rule thing again! I hope everyone will come to my party, but I don't want to get my hopes up...

Sunday, March 8

Dear Unhappy Birthday Journal,
Jill and Kelly called me today. It was the first time either has talked to me since February 13, and they both said they're going to their grandma's that weekend. I know they're lying. They just don't want to come to my birthday party!

When I told Mom, she said, "Don't let a couple of rude girls ruin your birthday. Let's see if Steph and Miranda can come, and if they can, then we'll plan something really special!"

Mom is so great sometimes. I hope she'll still have time to be great after the baby comes. There's only a couple months left!

Monday, March 9

Dear I-do-have-friends-after-all Journal,
Today at school both Steph and Miranda told me they can come to my party. I'm so relieved! At least I have two friends. I wasn't sure Steph would come, but I'm really glad she is. Miranda, too!

When I told Mom about them coming she said, "Great! This morning I saw an ad in the paper for an ice show at the University Arena that happens to be on March 13. The Olympic skating stars will be performing an exhibition there. We could make it a girls' night out... What do you think?"

"Yes!" I shouted. Things are starting to go my way. Kelly and Jill will be sorry when they hear about the ice show! (OOPS! I forgot about the Golden Rule. I mean, isn't it too bad that Kelly and Jill will be at their grandmas' and won't be able to go to the ice show with us?)

Saturday, March 14

Dear Happy Birthday Journal,
My birthday finally came, and this Friday the 13th wasn't bad at all, especially compared to February 13! Mom and Dad gave me this new outfit I've been wanting, and Mark got me some books. The baby gave me a watch. I thought that was weird. I mean, it isn't really here yet!

Mom, Steph, Miranda, and I had the best time at the skating exhibition. It was freezing sitting so close to the ice, but we forgot how cold we were when the skaters came out and glided past us. They did all of these amazing spins and jumps and stuff!

Little slivers of ice hit us when they skated close to our seats. We even got to go backstage for autographs – I got eleven signatures on my program! All the way home we talked about the ice show. This was a birthday party I'll always remember.

Then Mom asked, "I wonder if Kelly and Jill are having this much fun at their grandmas' houses."

"It serves them right," Steph added.

"See what happens when you lie?" Miranda said, laughing at the thought.

84

"I knew they were lying!" I said. "Oh well, too bad for them, huh?"

We had a lot of fun during the sleepover, too. We talked until three a.m. We talked about everything and everyone – even the disgusting Geoff Nelson.

"I can't stand him!" I said. "He still calls me Raccoon, and it's his fault I broke my nose in October."

"It was so gross when he barfed on your valentine mailbox!" Miranda added.

Steph was squirming in her sleeping bag. "Sorry I was mad at you about that, Sara. It wasn't your fault he threw up!" she said.

It felt good to hear Steph say that.

"I heard him say he was glad he wrecked your mailbox," Miranda told us.

"That big blubberhead! He's so mean, Sara!" Steph said angrily. "I'd like to teach him a lesson!"

"Hmmm. That gives me an extra crunchy idea!" I said. "April Fool's Day is coming up in a few weeks, right? Maybe we can think of a joke to play on Geoff!"

Miranda jumped out of her sleeping bag and danced around the room. "Listen to this!" she shrieked. "There's only one thing in the whole world that grosses out Geoff Nelson, and I know what it is!"

Steph and I stared at her in surprise.

She giggled, "You won't believe it!"

"What is it?" we begged.

"Worms!" she whispered.

"How do you know?" Steph asked, as I fell over laughing.

"One time in fourth grade Mike threw a worm at Geoff. He yelled his head off, and danced around trying to get it off. He was

so upset he had to go home for the rest of the day. It was too funny!"

"So what's your idea?" I demanded.

"My turtle eats worms, so I always have a supply around. We could hide some in Geoff's stuff!" she said.

"Yeah!" Steph agreed. "We could put some in his desk, and his backpack..."

"And his lunch box! Let's make him a worm sandwich!" I recommended.

"Let's call it Operation Slime Time!" Steph suggested. We hooted and howled with laughter, until I realized my parents' bedroom was right above us.

Waiting is the biggest problem. It's eighteen whole days until April 1! I guess that gives us time to get everything organized. I just don't know how we'll keep the secret. It has to be a total surprise, or it won't work, and then Geoff will find some new way to torture us as punishment! Help me keep our secret, Journal!

April

Wednesday, April 1

Dear Amnesty Journal,
Operation Slime Time was a huge success. All our plans went off without a hitch! For a while there I thought we were in big trouble, but it all worked out okay.

Steph, Miranda, and I got to school about fifteen minutes early. Miranda snuck inside to put the worms in Geoff's desk. Plan A had begun! Steph and I hung around by the swings while we waited for Miranda, but she never came out. When the bell rang for line-up, we were petrified that something had gone wrong!

As we walked into the building Steph and I were desperately hoping that Miranda hadn't been caught. We found her sitting at her desk with her math book out.

Miranda whispered that Mrs. Wood walked in right after she finished hiding the worms. She explained, "I told her I needed help multiplying fractions, so she made me do practice problems."

Just then Mrs. Wood made us sit down. She handed back our fraction tests and started explaining our grades. Suddenly...

"YEEOOWWWW!" Geoff screamed, and the fun began. He jumped out of his chair, knocking it over, and backed away from his desk. I knew we'd get a reaction, but I didn't know it would be this much fun!

"What is going on?" Mrs. Wood asked, rolling over to him.

He waved his arms, pointing and spluttering, "Look! Look in my desk!"

Everyone laughed (except Geoff and Mrs. Wood). She looked in Geoff's desk and pulled out three long, wiggling worms.

"YEEOOWWWW!" Geoff bellowed again. "Get those things away from me!"

He ran over to the reading corner.

Mrs. Wood was not happy. "Geoff, they aren't rattlesnakes. Please sit down and stop disrupting the class!" she demanded. Then she turned to the rest of us, holding up the worms. "Does anyone know how these got in Geoff's desk?"

"No, Mrs. Wood," we all said innocently.

Jill suggested, "He probably put them there himself!" Jill was still not speaking to me because of the Valentine's Day party. If she'd known she was helping us, she would have kept her mouth shut.

Mrs. Wood looked at Geoff suspiciously. "Well, Geoff?"

"Don't look at me!"

I thought, "Don't look at Miranda either!" Her guilty face was bright red.

Mrs. Wood put the worms in one of the plants we were growing on the windowsill. "Sorry. Let's just say I'm suspicious." Her eyebrow arched accusingly.

After math was over, Mrs. Wood had us take out our novels for silent reading.

Time for my part, Plan B! I was scared to death I'd mess it up. I asked to get my book out of my backpack, and Mrs. Wood said it was okay. I walked over to the coat rack and dug around in my backpack. When my hand closed on the bag of worms, I almost yelled myself! I looked around, but no one was paying any attention. I grabbed Geoff's lunch box, popped it open, shook the plastic bag until the worms dropped in, and snapped the lunch box shut again.

"Sara, are you finding everything okay back there?" Mrs. Wood asked. Yikes! Did she see what I was doing?

"Uh, yes. My book's right here," I said, fishing it out of my pack, while I shoved the plastic bag back in my pocket.

I opened my novel and tried to keep my mind on my book. I was dying for lunchtime to roll around so we could see what Geoff would do next. Would he give a repeat performance?

In fifteen minutes, it was time for Plan C, and it was Steph's turn to go to her backpack. No one else noticed, but Miranda and I had our eyes glued to her. We watched Steph dump worms from a plastic bag into Geoff's backpack. She threw the bag in the trash, sat down on the reading rug, and grinned at Miranda and me.

"You seem a little distracted, Sara," Mrs. Wood said, startling me completely.

"I'm just hungry," I answered quickly, and forced myself to act calm.

"Only ten minutes until lunchtime," she said. Mrs. Wood is no dummy, and I'm sure she knew something weird was going on, but thankfully she didn't make me tell her what it was.

Finally Mrs. Wood dropped us off at the cafeteria. Plan D began: the three of us sat in a row facing Geoff and Mike's usual seats. We weren't going to miss one glorious moment of Operation Slime Time!

We listened to their conversation. Mike said, "I've got bologna today. Wanna trade?"

"Maybe," Geoff answered, opening his lunch box.

"What do you have?" Mike asked, looking over Geoff's shoulder.

"YEEOOWWWW!" Geoff shrieked again, louder than ever! He tossed his lunch box straight up in the air, and a couple of the slimy worms landed on Geoff's shirt. He screamed again and jumped up, grabbed a

napkin, danced around, and tried to brush them off. For a few priceless seconds the worms were stuck to him, but then they fell on the floor, too. By this time the entire cafeteria was trying to see what was going on.

Suddenly Mrs. Smith, the lunch lady, appeared beside Geoff. Everyone froze.

"What in the world are you doing?" she demanded with her hands on her hips.

Geoff crawled around on the floor trying to pick up the parts of his lunch. "Somebody put w... bugs in my lunch box!"

"Um-hmm. And I wonder who that somebody was? Why don't you just take your lunch box to Mrs. Fellows' office and tell her all about it?" she ordered, walking Geoff to the door.

Everybody burst into laughter as Geoff stumbled out. And the day wasn't over yet.

We didn't see Geoff again until after Science. As he walked in and handed Mrs. Wood a note, his face looked like a thundercloud about to burst into a rainstorm. "Mrs. Fellows thinks I put... bugs in my lunch box, but I didn't! Somebody's playing April Fool's jokes on me!"

Mrs. Wood smiled slightly. "Geoff, I'm sad

 to say that people might be reluctant to believe you. You see, you've earned quite a reputation for pulling these kinds of pranks."

And that's when the rainstorm began. "But I really didn't do it! Why don't you search everybody's desks and see who's doing this to me?" he asked, tears welling up in his eyes. I've never seen Geoff Nelson cry before!

Mrs. Wood searched his face. "All right," she said. "I'll give you a chance to prove your innocence. Boys and girls, please take everything out of your desks and pile it on top so Geoff and I can have an inspection."

Thank goodness we didn't have anything in our desks to give us away! I calmly followed Mrs. Wood's instructions. She and Geoff walked around the room and looked into each desk, then looked through the stack of junk on top.

Mrs. Wood said to Geoff, "Except for that muddy spot in your desk, I don't see any evidence of worms."

I snickered and stole a glance at Steph, who was holding her breath like she always does when she's trying not to laugh.

Then Geoff got a weird look. "Hey, can we check the backpacks, too?" he suggested. "They might be in there!"

Mrs. Wood sighed. "All right, Geoff. But this is it! We're not spending our whole day worrying about your worms! Does anyone object to me looking in their backpacks?"

We were still okay – I was glad we had put the worms in plastic bags so our backpacks weren't muddy!

Mrs. Wood looked through each one. Finally she came to the last backpack. It was Kelly's, and she had no worms, of course. "What about your backpack, Geoff?" Kelly asked. (She is so brilliant, even if she is a bagel brain sometimes!)

He looked at her, and she said, "Well?"

"I've got nothing to hide!" Geoff dumped his backpack out on his desk. We knew what was coming next... the anticipation was almost as much fun as the screaming!

"YEEOOWWWW!"

Mrs. Wood sighed as she picked up another pile of worms. She took them to another plant and dropped them in, and then wiped her hands off on a tissue. When she went to throw it away, she stopped and stared into the garbage.

Geoff was dancing around his desk again. "I didn't do it! Somebody else put them in there, really! They aren't mine!"

Mrs. Wood ignored him. She reached down and dug through the trash. Geoff was still jabbering.

"Listen, Mrs. Wood! It's true! I would never bring those things to school! I hate them." He shivered.

Mrs. Wood was holding a dirty plastic bag in her hand. "Geoff, would you please show me the plastic bags you packed your lunch in today?"

"Why?" he asked.

"Just do what I say."

He pulled out two zipper sandwich bags.

"Look at this bag. What do you notice?" Mrs. Wood asked.

"It's muddy," he answered. Banana brain!

"Besides that," Mrs. Wood said. "Notice the way it closes."

Geoff looked again. "It doesn't zip shut, it just folds over."

"Exactly! Your family uses a different kind of bag. That must mean you're telling the truth, and someone else has been playing a joke on you."

Why was Mrs. Wood so good at solving mysteries? If we'd had a dumber teacher we might have gotten away with it!

Mrs. Wood told us to take out a piece of paper and a pencil and write her a note telling what we knew about the worm problem. She said if we confessed she'd give us amnesty. Mrs. Wood then explained, "Amnesty means pardoning or forgiving. If you write me a note confessing your guilt, I'll grant you amnesty. Your only punishment will be apologizing to Geoff for what you did today. Does that seem fair?"

We all wrote quickly. Thinking about my too-long, get-myself-in-more-trouble bathroom door letter, I wrote Mrs. Wood a short note this time:

Dear Mrs. Wood,
I did it.
Sara

I was the first one done. I folded my note in half and laid it on Mrs. Wood's desk. Steph was second, and Miranda was fourth or fifth. Other people were still writing, and I wondered what was taking them so long, since they weren't guilty.

Mrs. Wood didn't look up as she read the notes, but in a few minutes she went back to the front of the room.

"Before we leave today, I'd like to thank each of you for your honesty," she said.

Geoff asked anxiously, "Did you find out who did it?"

"Yes, I did. There were three people involved." That must mean Steph and Miranda told the truth, too! I was relieved even though I knew we were busted.

Mrs. Wood continued, "One person said that this was a terrible joke to play on you. Four people didn't know anything about it. Six people wrote that they can bring more worms, if anyone wants to do this again. And seven other people wrote they thought it was about time you got a taste of your own medicine. What do you think that means, Geoff?"

"Everybody's after me!" he squeaked.

When the final bell rang, Mrs. Wood had Geoff, Miranda, Steph, and me stay after. Geoff sat as far away from us as he could. "Well, this has been quite a day, hasn't it?" Mrs. Wood asked. "What's going on, girls?"

Miranda spoke first. "We wanted to play an April Fool's joke on Geoff, and I knew what he was afraid of. It was all my idea."

Steph quickly said, "But Sara and I wanted to do it, too."

"Why did you choose Geoff to play a joke on?" Mrs. Wood asked.

"He's always so mean to everyone, and he calls me Raccoon when he's the one who made me break my nose, and he barfed on my valentine mailbox, and..." I said, counting off the grievances on my fingers.

"I think we could call this revenge," Mrs. Wood suggested. She is so smart! Then she had me tell Geoff how we wanted him to treat us in the future.

"Okay," I started slowly. "We wanted to get even with you because you're such a bully. We want you to leave us alone, and

101

everybody else, too. We're sick of the way you treat us," I finished loudly.

Mrs. Wood broke in, "All right, Sara. I promised you amnesty, didn't I? Will you apologize to Geoff for the group?"

I said, "Sorry, Geoff."

He got up and left immediately. Mrs. Wood sighed and looked at the rug. Then

she said, "Hurry home before your parents get worried, girls." That was it! No lecture, no visits to Mrs. Fellows, no phone calls home – amnesty! What a great word!

I was surprised to see Jill and Kelly waiting for us on the playground. "Sara, we've been mean to you since the party, and we're sorry," Kelly apologized. "We want to be friends again."

"Your April Fool's joke was great!" Jill laughed. "I'll never forget the look on Geoff's face when he opened his lunch box!"

Kelly added, "Now everybody knows the magic word to make Geoff leave us alone."

"WORMS!" we shouted.

May

Wednesday, May 6

Dear Baby Contest Journal,
Tonight Mom was sitting in the family room with her swollen feet propped up on a footstool. They're big, but they're tiny compared to her huge stomach! I can't believe it doesn't hurt to have your skin stretch so far! Mom's stomach still doesn't have a name, after all our months of brainstorming. So Dad proposed a contest.

"Okay, let's each guess when the baby will be born, and whoever comes closest will win the contest and get to name the baby." Sometimes Dad surprises me with his coolness. None of my friends with little brothers and sisters got to name them!

Poor Mom's terrified the baby will get some horrible name, like "Napoleon" or "Fifi," so she wants veto power. I guess I can't blame her – who knows what Mark would pick if he won?

Mom picked her date first, since she's the one having the baby. She chose May twenty-fifth since that's her actual due date. How boring!

When it was my turn, I could not decide on a day. Finally I picked the eleventh, since I'm eleven. Mom about fainted because the eleventh is less than a week away.

Mark picked the sixth, because he's almost six. He's so dumb! Today's the sixth!

Dad chose the twenty-fourth, which shuts Mom out, unless the baby comes late.

After our family meeting, I raced for The Baby Name Encyclopedia. I want to find the perfect name – just in case I win. It will have to be easy to spell and pronounce. It also has to sound strong, not wimpy. And I think this baby should be able to have a nickname if it wants one. This is the most important thing I've ever decided!

Luckily the baby isn't due for weeks, so we still have a lot of time to decide on Baby Burnett's official name.

Saturday, May 16

Dear Labor Pains Journal,
Today we went to the championship game of Mark's baseball tournament. Dad, as usual, was shouting at Mark from the bleachers. Mom, as usual, was begging him to let the real coaches do their job. And I was trying to get interested in the billionth game I've had to watch Mark play.

Things got interesting when Mark hit a triple in the bottom of the ninth, and his team won by one run! We were all jumping around, hugging each other, when Mom collapsed onto the bleachers, grabbing her humongous stomach. At first I didn't get what was happening, but when she cried, "I think I'm in labor!" I knew we were in trouble.

Somehow or other, Dad managed to get Mom to the car. I grabbed Mark and tried to keep up. Mom kept trying to smile at us to keep us from worrying, but I could tell labor was no picnic.

Dad drove home from the ballpark in record time. No one said a word until we got to our next-door neighbors' driveway. Dad leaped out of the car and pounded on their door. When they opened it, he explained the situation and asked  them to keep an eye on us. Then he turned to me and said, "Sara, I'm taking Mom to the hospital. Call Grandma and Grandpa and tell them to come now!" He looked totally flustered as he drove away again.

I ran inside and called Grandma and Grandpa. They've been planning to stay with us at the end of May, when Mom's supposed to have the baby.

"Grandma? Dad told me... and poor Mom... and can you come?" I babbled.

"Steady, Sara. Is your mom having the baby?" Grandma asked quietly.

"Yes!"

She said, "Grandpa and I will be there within the hour. Just stay calm, okay?"

Yeah, right. I haven't been calm for nine whole months!

When Grandma and Grandpa came, they brought us dinner. While we ate, we told them all about the game and about Mom.

We got out all our board games and spent the evening playing. It was really hard to concentrate on the games. I was so busy worrying about Mom that I accidentally let Mark beat me at checkers!

Grandma and Grandpa made us go to bed a little while ago. There's no way I can sleep with all of the excitement!

108

Sunday, May 17

Dear Forgotten Birthday Journal,
When I woke up this morning my clock said 8:45 - I couldn't believe I slept so late! I ran down to the kitchen and found Grandma and Grandpa drinking coffee and reading the Sunday paper.

"Did they call? Did Mom have the baby yet?" I asked excitedly.

"I called the hospital, but they wouldn't connect me to her room. I think that's a good sign!" Grandma answered.

"Why?" I asked.

"It could mean she's finally having the baby, and they're too busy to talk to us."

"So we still don't know anything," I muttered. "I can't stand the suspense!"

"We'll stop by this afternoon, okay?" Grandma said. "In the meantime, let's get the house clean and ready for your mom. Time passes more quickly when you're busy."

"You keep saying that, but I think time has stopped completely!" I complained.

Finally the house was cleaned. Finally Grandpa drove us to the hospital. Finally we'd know something!

The man at the information desk checked his computer and told us Mom was in room 715. "Does it say if she's had the baby yet?" Grandma asked.

He looked again. "Yes, she has."

"Hooray!" Mark cheered loudly, so I clapped my hand over his mouth.

"Is it a boy or a girl?" I whispered.

"I don't have that information," the man explained. "You'll have to check on that yourselves."

When we got there, we tiptoed down the hall until we came to room 715. Grandpa was just about to knock on the door when Dad pushed it open. He had bloodshot eyes and Albert Einstein hair. He looked terrible!

But we weren't there to see Dad, so we pushed past him into Mom's room. She was propped up in bed, with a little plastic baby bed next to her. She looked tons better than she did the last time I saw her! She must have taken a shower, because her hair was still wet, and she had a big, beautiful smile across her entire face.

"Long time no see," she told us, holding out her arms. "I couldn't wait to see you two!" I was so glad to see her, too, and so relieved she seemed to feel better. Mark and I hugged her carefully.

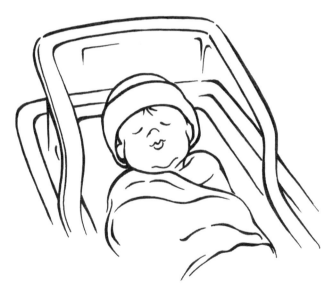

"Didn't I tell you everything was going to be okay?" she asked us. We nodded.

Grandma said, "What's the baby's name?"

Dad said, "That's up to Sara."

Grandma and Grandpa looked confused until Mark explained our baby contest.

"I picked the eleventh, so I guess that makes me closest," I said. "But I haven't picked my names yet!" Panic hit — I have a huge responsibility ahead of me!

Mom said, "That's all right. We don't want to rush and choose the wrong name."

Mark finally lost his patience. "Hey, did you get me a brother or not?"

"Not," Dad said, putting his hands on Mark's shoulders and smiling down at him. "We're outnumbered now, buddy."

"Aw, rats," he grumbled.

"Yes!" I cheered. "Three to two!"

Mom got out of bed and showed us the baby. I can't believe how tiny she is! She only weighs six pounds, eight ounces, because she was born early. She has tons of black hair that sticks straight out. We can't really tell what color her eyes are yet because she doesn't open them much.

We stayed in Mom's room for over an hour, passing the baby around and listening to the story of how she was born. It doesn't sound like much fun to me!

Mark was pouting. He wouldn't hold the baby, or even look at her. Finally he talked Grandpa into taking us out for burgers.

All four of us were starving. Grandpa let us get whatever we wanted, which was extra crunchy! We couldn't finish our chocolate milkshakes, so we took them home in the car.

When we got home, there were six little boys wearing super hero costumes and a bunch of parents sitting on our front step. I gasped, "Today is Mark's birthday! We forgot all about his birthday party, too!"

"Hey, today is my birthday!" Mark remembered. He had a new reason to pout. "This morning nobody gave me a present, or sang 'Happy Birthday' or anything!"

We explained about the baby, then herded all the little boys into the living room. Grandpa went off to buy cake and ice cream. Mark and his buddies watched a video while we got everything ready.

Grandma and I worked fast to blow up balloons, hang streamers, and set the table. We were afraid cake and ice cream weren't enough for six hungry little boys, so I got out the phone book and ordered pizza.

Somehow we survived the birthday party. It took all three of us to keep the boys busy and having fun. It was hard work, but for once I didn't mind helping Mark. I'd be really sad if no one remembered my birthday! We might have forgotten Mark's birthday for a little while, but from now on, we'll always remember this exciting day. And now we have two May 17 birthdays - Mark and the baby are birthday twins! I bet Mark hasn't figured that out yet.

Monday, May 18

Dear Hopeless Contest Journal,
When I went to school today, I told Mrs. Wood about the new baby and the agonies I was having naming her. She suggested having everyone brainstorm some names for me. I agreed, thinking that it might help.

Mrs. Wood explained the naming contest to the class, and called on kids when they had suggestions. I wrote down their ideas. Some of them were goofy, but a few were pretty good. There are too many possibilities to choose from!

After school, Grandma and Grandpa picked Mark and me up so we could go visit Mom and the baby. Dad says they get to come home tomorrow! While we were there, I spent most of my time holding the baby. The more I see her, the more I want to hold her, and the more I hold her, the more I like her! It's kind of scary to discover I actually like this baby! Mark, on the other hand, ignored her completely.

Mom gave me a little smile and asked, "Do you think Mark is going to be okay with having a sister?"

"Don't worry. He'll get used to her when you come home." I hope I'm right. If not, it could be World War III at our house!

"I hope so. So, have you decided what your sister's name is going to be, honey?" Mom asked, holding out her arms.

I carefully handed the sleeping baby back to her. "I don't know yet. The kids at school helped me brainstorm today, and I've been looking in the name book. There are just too many choices!"

"Dad and I will help you if you just can't decide," she said.

I told her I'll think about it again tonight. We get to stay home from school tomorrow for the big homecoming, and if I haven't thought of a name by then, I'll let Mom and Dad name the baby.

When we got home, I spent the whole evening poring through The Baby Name Encyclopedia. Finally, at ten o'clock, I had to go to bed. Grandma asked me if I had narrowed it down to a few favorite names. I have about twenty! I'm ready to give up.

Tuesday, May 19

Dear Eureka Journal,
When I woke up this morning it was all clear! I know the perfect name for our new sister. I'm so relieved! I'm not quite ready to tell anyone else – not yet. I'll wait until we get to the hospital and tell Mom and Dad first. Then I'll tell you tonight!

Still Tuesday, May 19

Dear Welcome Home Journal,
I DID IT! I finally named the baby! Once everyone was gathered at the hospital, Mom held my sister out to me, and I carefully supported her tiny head with my elbow. I cleared my throat and announced, "After a lot of thinking – a lot of thinking – I decided the baby's name will be Catherine, and we'll call her Kate."

"I love it, Sara! It's perfect," Mom said.

She and Dad smiled at each other. "But what about her middle name?" he asked.

"Kate"

"Elizabeth, after Grandma," I explained.

Everyone loves the name Catherine Elizabeth, except Mark. He, of course, says he hates it. Surprise, surprise.

Wednesday, May 27

Dear Chaos Journal,

Things have been so crazy since Mom and Kate got home from the hospital! It's taking a while for us to adjust to having another kid around, especially one that's up all night.

The first Saturday Kate was home, the weirdest thing happened: Mark's friends

119

kept parading into the house and asking Mom, "Can I see your baby?"

At first we thought it was kind of cute, but by the fourth time, we were tired of the doorbell ringing. I decided to get out of the house for a few minutes and check the mail. As I walked down the driveway, I noticed a little white sign on a stick by the curb. I went closer to investigate. Mark's crooked handwriting read:"

See the Alien Baby only 25¢

"MOM!" I shouted. I grabbed the sign and ran back to the house.

Mom held the door open for me. "What's the matter?"

"Read this!" I shrieked.

She sighed, then handed Kate to me and headed up the stairs to Mark's room. She went in and closed the door behind her.

In less than a minute, Mark's four friends dashed down the steps and out the front door.

Then Mom came into the family room with Mark right behind her. "Kate is not an alien baby!" she said.

"They didn't know that," he said.

Mom sighed and asked Mark, "Why are you acting this way?"

"I just thought it would be funny," he answered sullenly.

"I don't think that's it." Then a lightbulb went off in Mom's head. "You know, I don't think you've even held Kate yet."

"Aw, Mom, I might drop her or something," he said nervously.

"Sit down right there on the couch. Don't move!" she said softly. She took Kate from me and laid her across Mark's lap, showing him how to support Kate's neck.

Mark looked down at Kate. As he stared at her, a smile burst across her tiny face.

"Wow! Did you see that? She smiled at me! Do you think she... likes me?" he asked.

"Of course she does!" Mom said.

"Can you smile again, Kate?" he asked in a goofy voice. "Give your favorite brother a big smile."

It's all over. Kate wrapped Mark around her little finger already! It's amazing how powerful a week-old baby can be!

June

Friday, June 5

Dear Final Pages Journal,

I can't believe it! I just looked and you only have three pages left, Journal. Just think about everything I've written to you over the past crazy nine months: I broke my nose, I created my own punishment, I had a job, I got revenge on Geoff Nelson with worms, and I have a new sister.

Best of all, because I have recorded all of this, I'm never going to forget it! I'm going to miss you, Journal, but I've enjoyed having you to confide in so much that I've decided to go out and buy Journal II.

I guess one of the coolest things is that money isn't going to be a problem for me again. I have a weekend job all lined up - what a relief! I figured Mom was going to have me babysit, but instead she said she'll pay me to be the cleaning lady when she starts working at home in a couple weeks. Maybe I'll start saving my money now so I can buy presents next December.

Kate is almost a month old already. She is, without a doubt, the best baby in the entire world! She hardly ever cries anymore. Her smiles melt my heart (Mark's too!), and the way her eyes and nose crinkle up is adorable!

Mark has taken to calling Kate his baby. He hardly lets anyone else hold her or play with her. Sometimes I want a turn, too!

I just looked back at what I wrote on the first page in my journal last September. I can't believe what a total blubberhead I was when Mom and Dad told us about the baby! But I was terrified. I was sure Mark and I had let our parents down somehow, and they were having another baby so they'd have a better kid. Back then, when I was younger, all I knew was I didn't want Mom to have another baby. Today it's so easy to understand what I was feeling way back then. Wow – I must be growing up!

Well, I can't believe that this is your last page, journal! It's been great writing to you, my extra crunchy friend. You were always there, keeping my secrets about the good, the bad, and everything else in my life. Thanks! Bye!

From the Author

I'm an elementary school teacher in Colorado. I've always loved children's books, and I wanted to write a funny story that neither kids nor teachers would want to put down. All in all, it took ten years for this book to be born. More than 1,000 kids gave me the suggestions I needed to polish my writing.

Some chapters were revised almost thirty times, others only nine or ten. I want to give monumental thanks to all of the Douglas County and Cherry Creek students who listened, advised, and inspired me. I couldn't have done it without them.

In addition, Marjory Ulm read my drafts and helped me find Sara's voice. My doctor friends, Michael Hunt and Ken Katz, helped me with my medical research for Sara's October entries. I couldn't have done it without them, either.

Last of all, it's important to thank my "extra crunchy" family for their support: my husband, Kim; my son, Ross; and my own Catherine Elizabeth. Without their encouragement, this book would still be just a dream.

Ann Trunnell Herrell

From the Illustrator

For the past fifteen years I've been an illustrator and designer in Chicago. I live with my husband, Nik, and my dog, Bosco, in Hillside, Illinois. Bosco sits on my desk as I draw and is a good companion. We enjoy music, traveling, hiking, and chasing mail trucks. Well... Bosco likes to chase mail trucks. We end up chasing him.

While reading this book, I tried to imagine what the characters were feeling and how it would make them look. Sometimes I would peer into a mirror and ask myself how would Steph frown when she wore her sister's princess costume. Or, how would anger shoot from Sara's eyes when she thought of Geoff Nelson.

The most important thing in becoming an illustrator, besides talent and perseverance, is people who believe in you. I'd like to thank my mom for saying, "You can do it," throughout my life and my sister, Sharon, for sharing her love of children's books. And most of all, I thank Nik, whose constant love and admiration gets me through most days.

Katherine Klimt

© Text by **Ann Trunnell Herrell**
Illustrated by **Katherine Klimt**
Edited by **Rebecca McEwen**
Designed by **Karen Baxa Hoglund**

04 03 02 01 00
10 9 8 7 6 5 4 3 2

Distributed in the United States by
    RIGBY
    a division of Reed Elsevier Inc.
    P.O. Box 797
    Crystal Lake, IL 60039-0797

Printed in Hong Kong.
ISBN: 0-7699-0415-7